The Reason for the Season

Story by Chantal Ellen

Illustrations by Phillip Pierre-Louis

To Mommy and Nadia, my pancake, for inspiring this story.
And to Sophia and Natalia, the most precious little ones I know.

—*Chantal Ellen*

To my mother, Gabrielle, for her love, support and guidance.

—*Phillip Pierre-Louis*

Text copyright © Chantal Ellen

Illustrations copyright © Phillip Pierre-Louis

Published by Cub Collection, an imprint of Lions Den Publishing. Manufactured in China.

Library of Congress Control Number: 2007926040

ISBN 13 - 978-0-9786786-1-6

ISBN 10 - 0-9786786-1-3

CUB COLLECTION, *Washington DC*

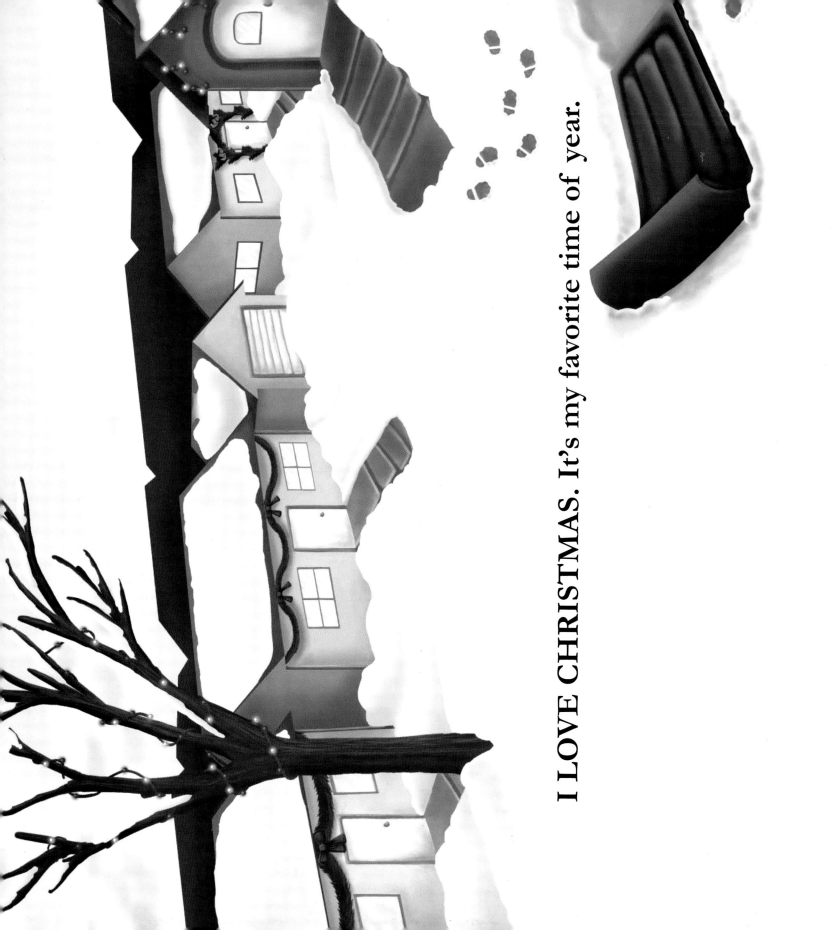

I LOVE CHRISTMAS. It's my favorite time of year.

I love spending time with everyone who comes to visit.

I love the decorations. I always get to put the star at the top of our Christmas tree.

Most of all, I love getting presents.

This year, Grandma asked,
"Do you know the true meaning of Christmas?"

I thought for a minute. "Christmas is a time for giving," I said, "so that all children can get presents." Grandma laughed. "No, that's not it," she said.

I thought harder. "Christmas is about spreading holiday cheer. That's why we have Christmas lights and Christmas trees."

"No, that isn't it either," she said.

I scratched my head and thought really, really, really hard. "Oh, I know! Christmas is about spending time with family and friends."

Grandma shook her head. "No, dear, although I love that part, too."

"Then why do we celebrate Christmas, Grandma?" I asked.

"Christmas is the day we celebrate the birth of baby Jesus," she explained.

"Oh," I said, starting to feel sad.

"Why the long face?" Grandma asked.

"I'm sad because Christmas isn't any of the things I love most about it," I said.

"Do you know the story of the birth of baby Jesus?" she asked.

"No," I answered.

"Well, let me tell you all about it," Grandma said, pulling me onto her lap.

"Many, many years ago, in a town called Bethlehem, baby Jesus was born in a stable. He was placed in a manger filled with hay. Now, Jesus is the Son of God, so his birth was very special.

An angel told shepherds about it, and they traveled to Bethlehem to visit baby Jesus.

Baby Jesus was also visited by wise men, who had been guided by a new and brightly shining star that hung high in the sky.

They brought baby Jesus gifts and worshipped Him because He was born to save the world."

I smiled at Grandma. "I like that story," I said.

"I'm glad," she said. "Can you see how we came to have the Christmas traditions you love so much?"

"How?" I asked.

"You like when friends and family come to visit.
What does that remind you of?"

I thought really hard and said, "Umm... the shepherds and the wise men visiting baby Jesus?"

"That's right," she said.

"What about the decorations—the lights and the star you put at the top of the Christmas tree?"

"Oh, I know," I said, "that's like the bright star that led the wise men to baby Jesus."

"Right again," she said.

"And what about your most favorite thing of all: Christmas gifts?"

"That's easy, Grandma. That's like when the wise men brought gifts to baby Jesus."

"And right again!" she said.

"All these things are wonderful and they make the holiday fun, but always remember that the birth of baby Jesus is the reason for the season."

I gave my grandma a great, big hug. "I'll never forget, Grandma," I promised. "I'll never forget."